Molly Maybe

For Poppylulu Herbertson, with love K.S.

SIMON AND SCHUSTER
First published in Great Britain in 2016
by Simon and Schuster UK Ltd
1st Floor, 222 Gray's Inn Road, London WC1X 8HB
A CBS Company

ISBN: 978-1-4711-2110-4 (PB)
ISBN: 978-1-4711-2111-1 (eBook)

Printed in China

1 3 5 7 9 10 8 6 4 2

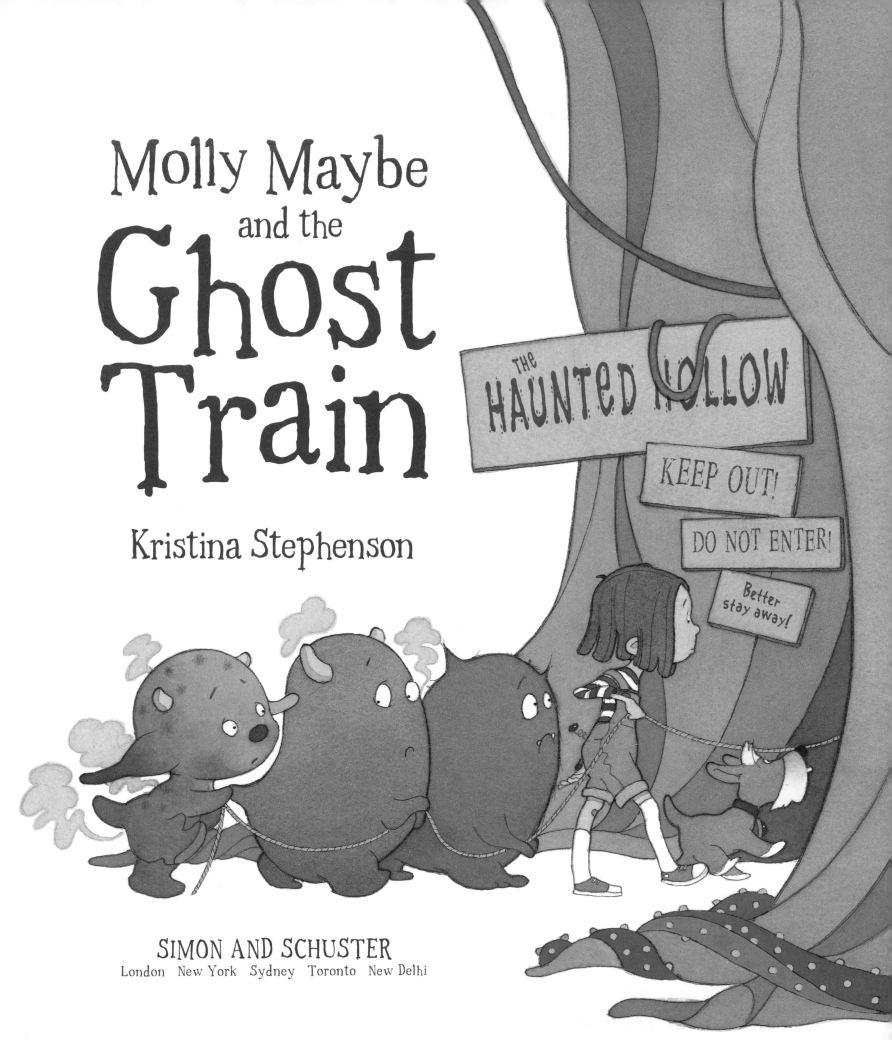

Molly Maybe
and the
Ghost
Train

Kristina Stephenson

THE HAUNTED HOLLOW

KEEP OUT!

DO NOT ENTER!

Better stay away!

SIMON AND SCHUSTER
London   New York   Sydney   Toronto   New Delhi

It was early morning
in Smallsbury.

Molly Maybe was
up in her tree house
with her dog,
Waggy Burns.

They were taking it in
turns with a paintbrush
when they smelt
A TERRIBLE SMELL.

'Pooh! Was that you?' asked Molly.
'Woof, woof, woof!' said Waggy, pointing to Mr Buster-Pipe,
the drain cleaner, who was driving into town.
'Oh!' said Molly. 'The drains must be blocked.'

By the end of the day Mr Buster-Pipe
was finished but the smell was worse than before.

'Maybe it's not the drains,' said Molly thoughtfully.
She took down a large book and read for a few moments.
'Listen to this,' she said to Waggy Burns.
'When monsters are frightened they give off a pong.'

BIG BOOK OF
MONSTERS

'If the monsters are scared,' said Molly, 'we need to find out why.
It's time to go underground Waggy Burns.'
Waggy wiggled his wiry whiskers and waggled off to fetch
his special Walkie-Talkie Collar.

Then Molly
opened a door
in the tree house floor
and they climbed
aboard the...

Down,

...MUNDERVATOR.

You see Molly had an amazing secret.

Her tree house led to a monster world deep beneath the ground and this marvellous, moving, mechanical machine was the only way to get there.

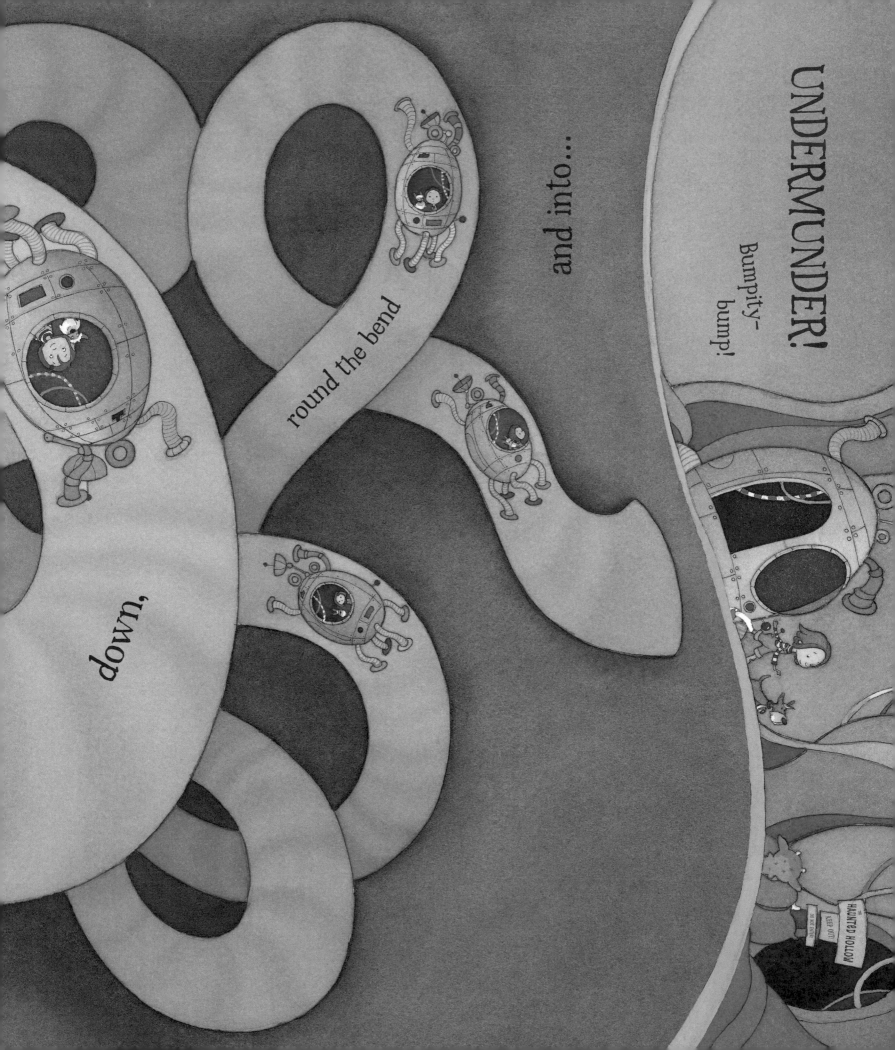

down,

round the bend

and into...

UNDERMUNDER!

Bumpity-bump!

THE HAUNTED HOLLOW
KEEP OUT!
DO NOT ENTER

The Mundervator had arrived at the edge of The Haunted Hollow where three terrified little monsters were pumping out a pong.

'Woof, woof, woof,' said Waggy Burns, trying to tell Molly something.

Molly switched on his Walkie-Talkie Collar so her clever companion could speak.

THE HAUNTED HOLLOW

KEEP OUT!

DO NOT ENTER!

Better stay away!

'I've come to the canine conclusion,' said Waggy, 'we've found the source of the smell.'

'Whatever's the matter?' said Molly to the monsters.
'Our kite crashed so we followed the string to find out where
it landed,' said the monsters. 'But we're too scared to go
any further because of the GHOULIE GUMPUS.'

'What's a Ghoulie Gumpus?' asked Molly.

'He's a ghastly ghost,' said the little monsters, shivering.
'He lives in The Haunted Hollow but no one's ever seen him, because
no one dares go in there in case the Gumpus GETS THEM!'

'Golly!' whispered Molly to Waggy. 'No wonder there's a smell of fear.'

'Indeed,' said Waggy, 'but I have a hunch
things are not what they seem.'

Molly thought for a moment or two then she turned to the little monsters.

'If you want to get your kite back, you'll have to go into that hollow. Why don't Waggy and I go with you?

We're not afraid of ghosts.
And, besides,' she said,
with a twinkle in her eye,
'sometimes scary can be FUN!'

The monsters weren't entirely sure
but they did want to get
their kite back.

So they picked up the string
and followed Molly into
The Haunted Hollow.

THE HAUNTED HOLLOW

KEEP OUT!

DO NOT ENTER!

Better
stay away!

The sound echoed down the abandoned mine and something stirred inside...

Tippety-toe, tippety-toe.

They followed the string past an abandoned mine, as quietly as tiny mice, and they would have got by without any trouble except...

... one of the monsters tripped -

oomph!

- over some track and into a cart.

Clackity, clackity, clack!

Bats burst out, swooping and looping.
The monsters shivered and shook.

But Molly took them by their paws
and together they ventured on.

They pushed their way through creepy cobwebs that hung in a gruesome graveyard.

Ooooh!

B A GHOUL

SKELLY BONES

R.I.P

They squealed and reeled when they saw scary spiders scuttling across the floor.

Shriek!

They dipped
and ducked
under claw-like
branches.

But they
STOPPED
when they got
to the end of the string
and they saw...

Yikes!

And they scurried
past the rats.

Eeeek!

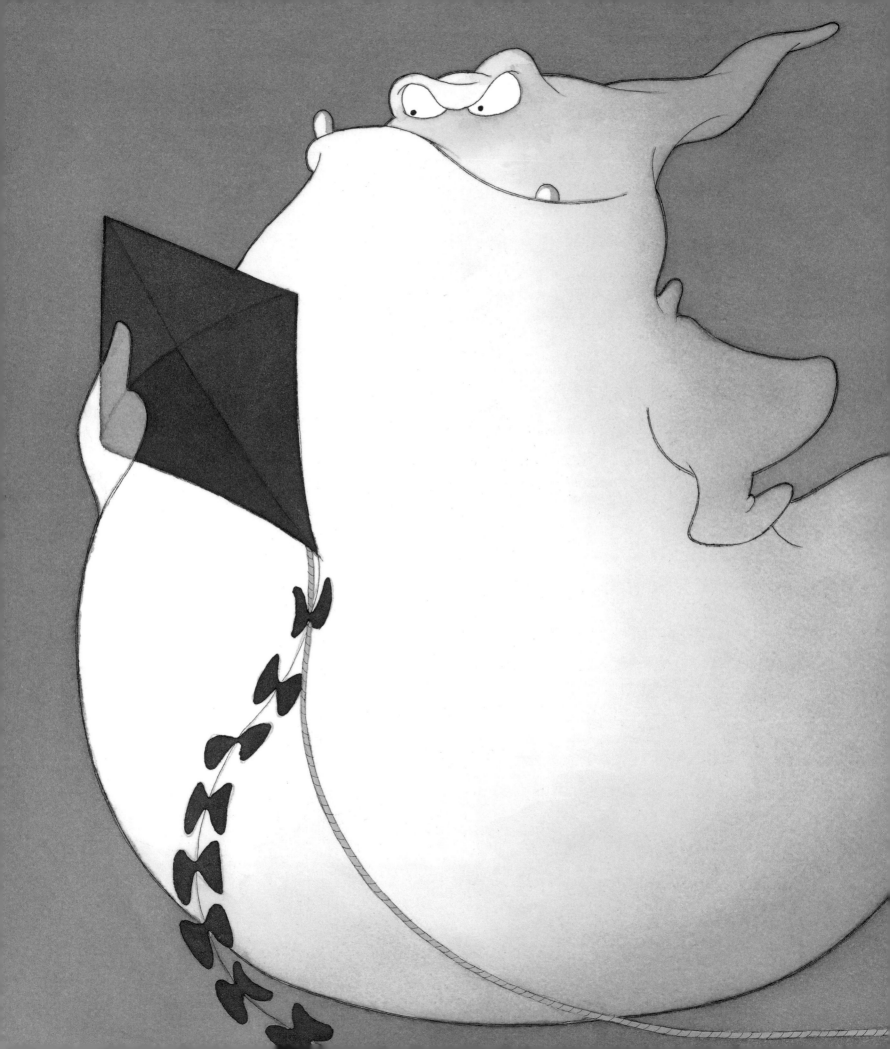

...the Ghoulie Gumpus!

'Aaaaahhh! The Gumpus!'
screamed the terrified little monsters,
pumping out a mighty pong.

'AAAAAHHH! MONSTERS!'

screamed the ghost
quivering and quaking with fright.

'Gracious-good-golly!'
said Molly to the monsters.

'All this time you've been afraid of the Gumpus,
while he's been afraid of YOU.'

It didn't take long
for everyone to see there
was NOTHING to be scared of.

Waggy wiggled his whiskers again.

'If only ALL the monsters
could meet the Ghoulie
Gumpus,' he said.

'I'll hazard a hound-like guess
that everyone would get along.'
'But how do we get the others
in here,' said the little monsters,
'when no one in Undermunder
DARES to go into
The Haunted Hollow?'

Then Molly had an idea.

'The monsters
might come into
the hollow if
their CHILDREN
tell them to,'
she said.

Molly told the Ghoulie Gumpus and the little
monsters what she wanted them to do.

'You get to work,' she said with a smile.
'We'll be back in a bit.'

Then she and Waggy
raced through the hollow,
and climbed aboard
the Mundervator.

Down, down, round the bend and...

...back to Molly's tree house where her paints and brushes were waiting.

Molly and Waggy didn't stop work until they'd painted four new signs.

Then they took them back to The Haunted Hollow to see if the plan would work.

It did! In no time at all word got out about the fabulous…

GHOST TRAIN

CLIMB ABOARD

Everyone welcome!

FUN FUN FUN!

Every little monster
in Undermunder
wanted to take a ride.

They lined up with their
mums and dads, who bought
their tickets from the
Ghoulie Gumpus – such
a friendly ghost.

Then they...

Everyone had such FUN!

'Monster mission accomplished!' said Molly. Waggy wiggled his whiskers.

Early next morning,
up in Smallsbury,
Mr Buster-Pipe was back.

He was pleased
that the smell had gone
from the drains but...

...where had he left his hat?